WALT DISNEY's
Bambi
Snowy Day

Written by Betty Birney

Illustrated by David Pacheco
and Diane Wakeman

Cover illustrated by Francesc Mateu

A GOLDEN BOOK • NEW YORK

Golden Books Publishing Company, Inc., New York, New York 10106

One cold and frosty morning, Bambi woke up and could not believe his eyes! Overnight, everything in the forest had turned white!

Plop! Something cold and wet fell on Bambi's head.

"It's snow," said Thumper as he hopped toward Bambi. "That means it's winter. Let's go and play!"

"Okay," answered Bambi. "And we'll get Flower, too."

As Bambi and Thumper romped around in the woods, they noticed a set of footprints in the fluffy white snow.

"Those aren't *my* footprints. And they aren't *your* footprints," said Thumper. "Hey, maybe they're Flower's footprints!"

"Let's follow them and find out," suggested Bambi.

They followed the trail of footprints until it ended at the base of a hollow tree.

But instead of Flower, Bambi and Thumper found a family of opossums. "Hello, opossums!" they called.

The opossums came outside to say hello. Bambi explained that he and Thumper were looking for Flower. "Look! Here are some more footprints," shouted a young opossum. "These probably belong to Flower. I'll go with you and we'll find him in no time!"

The new footprints were much smaller than the first set.

"This is fun!" shouted Thumper. "These footprints hop all over the place, just like me!"

The three friends happily bounded along the zigzagging path until they almost hit their noses on a snow-covered tree stump.

There on top of the stump, sat a red cardinal.
"Hello," said Thumper to the cardinal. "Have you seen Flower?"
"No," said the cardinal shaking his head.

Then the cardinal chirped and hopped over to the other side of the stump. "Look over here!" he said excitedly.

"More footprints!" shouted Thumper. "Maybe these belong to Flower. Come on, everybody!"

Thumper led the others along the new trail of footprints to the top of a hill. Suddenly Thumper vanished from sight.

"Where did he go?" wondered Bambi as he scrambled to the top of the hill. Below him, Bambi saw Thumper standing on the pond. He couldn't **believe his eyes!**

"It's all right!" shouted Thumper. "The water's stiff." The little rabbit slid across the ice and did a twirl. "Come on, everybody. This is great!" Soon all four friends were slipping and sliding happily across the ice.

Suddenly, the little red cardinal began to chirp again.
"Maybe he's found more footprints!" suggested the
opossum.

He had indeed. So Bambi and his friends set off again in
hopes of finding Flower.

First the footprints led to a narrow stream that was almost hidden in the snow. Then they circled around the stream and led the friends to another hollow tree.

"Maybe we'll find Flower here," said Bambi.

The animals peeked into the hollow tree. But instead of Flower, they found a family of raccoons eating their breakfast. "Have you seen Flower?" Bambi asked.

The raccoons shook their heads. "I never saw a flower in the snow before," answered one raccoon. "But we will help you look for one."

The friends went outside to search for more footprints.
Then suddenly Friend Owl swooped down from the trees.
"What's the commotion?" he asked.

We're looking for Flower," explained Bambi.

"But every time we follow his footprints, they turn out to belong to somebody else," added Thumper.

Friend Owl chuckled. "You won't find Flower's footprints in the snow now. He's hibernating."

"Hibernating? What's that?" asked Bambi.

"Follow me," said Friend Owl.
He led Bambi and his friends through the snow to a hole at
the side of a hill. It was very quiet all around. Then they heard
a familiar soft snoring coming out of the opening.

The animals peered into the cozy den. There they saw Flower.
"Wake up! Wake up!" shouted Bambi and Thumper.
Flower opened one eye and yawned a big yawn.
"Is it spring yet?" he asked.
"No," said Bambi. "Winter is just beginning."

Flower yawned again. "Well, good night then," he said and was soon fast asleep.

"That's hibernating," Friend Owl explained. "He'll sleep until spring."

Suddenly the raccoons and the opossum began to yawn, too.

"That sounds like a very good idea," said the raccoons and the opossums sleepily. They wandered off home to catch a long winter's nap.

Bambi felt a little sad. "I'm going to miss our friends," he said to Thumper.

"Me too," said Thumper. Then he thought of something. "I know. We can go and play with all my brothers and sisters!"

"That's a great idea!" exclaimed Bambi.

The two friends soon found the rest of Thumper's family, and they all had many more wonderful winter adventures together!